STORYTIME TALES

Contents

STORYTIME
TALES

p

Home Sweet Home

Bella Bunny looked at the sweet green grass growing in the meadow on the far side of the stream. She was tired of eating the rough grass that grew near her burrow. "I'm going to cross the stream!" she said to her brothers and sisters, pointing to a fallen branch that lay across it.

Bella bounced safely across the branch and was soon eating the sweet, juicy grass on the other side of the stream. Her brothers and sisters thought she was very brave and wondered if they should follow. But just then, they saw a sly fox creeping up behind Bella through the grass!

"Look out!" they called.

Bella turned to see the fox just in time! She leapt back onto the branch, but she was in such a hurry that she slipped and fell into the stream. Luckily, Becky Beaver had been watching and she pulled Bella safely to the other side.

"Home sweet home!" gasped Bella, with relief. And she ran off to join her brothers and sisters, vowing never to leave home again.

Benny the Barmy Builder

Benny was a hard-working builder, and he always did his very best. But sometimes he could be forgetful!

One morning, Benny the Builder arrived bright and early at Vicky Vet's surgery. "Benny the Builder at your service!" he announced. "I think you have a job for me to do."

"Not me, Benny," replied Vicky. "But Polly Postlady has!"

"Of course!" said Benny. "Sorry – I really shouldn't be so forgetful!"

And off he went to Polly Postlady's house. "Benny the Builder at your service!" Benny announced. "Woof!" said Benny's dog, Rocky.

"Come in," called Polly.

She took out a drawing to show Benny.

"I want you to build a Wendy house in my garden," Polly said. "It's a surprise for my grandchildren, Peter, Penny and Patty. I did this drawing to

show you just how it should look."

Benny and Polly looked at the drawing together.

"The Wendy house should have two tall doors," said Polly, "one at the front and one at the back, with one small step at the back door. There should be five windows, one at either side of the front door and one on each of the other sides."

"Yes, I see," said Benny.

"And I want a nice sloping roof," said Polly, "not a flat roof!"

"Yes, I see," said Benny. "I will do my very best!"

Polly left for the post office, and Benny went out to start work. But he had barely begun when a gust of wind came along. WHOOSH! went Polly's drawing, up in the air. "WOOF!" barked Rocky, leaping up to catch it.

Oh no! The drawing got caught in the branches of a tree!

Rocky fetched the drawing but, by the time Benny got it back, it was in shreds.

"Oh dear!" moaned Benny the Builder.

"How will I build the Wendy house now?"

Benny tried to remember everything in the drawing. But he quickly got very confused!

"Was it five windows and two doors with one step?" Benny puzzled. "Or was it two windows and five doors with three steps? Was the roof flat and not sloping? Or sloping and not flat? Were the doors tall or small? Oh dear, oh dear!"

Benny decided that he would just have to do the best he could. He got to work measuring… mixing… laying bricks… sawing wood… hammering nails… fixing screws… plastering and painting… and doing his very best to make everything just right.

Late that afternoon, Polly Postlady got home from work. She couldn't wait to see what Benny had done. But, what a surprise she had! The Wendy house's roof was flat. The bottom of the house was sloping. There were two steps leading up to two doors on one side of the house and there were two floors, both different sizes. And there were two windows on one side of the house.

"It's all wrong!" said Polly to Benny. "How will you ever fix it in time?"

But Benny didn't have a chance to answer because, just at that moment, Polly's grandchildren arrived.

"Oooh! Look! A Wendy house!" they cried happily as they rushed towards it. "There's a door for each of us!" they all cried together.

"And we can climb right up to the roof!" said Patty.

"And slide down the other side!" said Peter.

"And there are loads of windows so it's nice and bright inside!" said Penny.

"Granny, it's the best Wendy house ever!" the children told Polly. "It is perfect. Thank you so much!"

"Well, I think you should thank Benny the Builder," said Polly Postlady, smiling. Benny the Builder smiled too. "I just did my very best," he said.

The New Cat

The cats on Old MacDonald's farm like nothing better than dozing. Milly just loves to laze in the sun, and Lazy, as his name suggests, hardly opens his eyes!

One day, Milly was snoozing on a bale of hay, when she heard Old MacDonald talking on the telephone through the open kitchen window. Half-asleep, she heard him say, "The new cat…" Milly was feeling very sleepy. "Yes," continued Old MacDonald, "I need it because the ones I have now are useless."

Milly yawned and stretched, still drowsy and happy. Then she suddenly sat bolt upright. What? The cats were useless? A new one was coming? Oh no!

Milly dashed to where Lazy was fast asleep and eventually woke him up! She hurriedly shouted what she had heard.

"What's the matter with us?" yawned Lazy in a hurt voice. "I don't understand."

"You don't do anything," clucked Henrietta the hen, who liked to put her beak into everybody's business. "You just sleep all day."

Milly and Lazy looked at each other. They knew there was only one thing to do. Ten seconds later, they were tearing around the farmyard, trying to look as busy as possible!

By the end of a week of dashing around all day and miaowing all night, the cats had created quite a stir in the farmyard.

"Look here," said Bruce the sheepdog. "What has got into you both?"

Milly and Lazy explained. Bruce tried not to smile. "Well, you're doing the right thing," he barked. "Impress Old MacDonald like this and you'll be fine. But I would stop the caterwauling at night."

Bruce strolled off chuckling to himself. As Old MacDonald's right-hand dog, he knew that the farmer was waiting for a new CATalogue to order his winter wellies from. But he didn't think he needed to tell Milly and Lazy that – not quite yet anyway!

Hazel Squirrel Learns a Lesson

Hazel Squirrel had the finest tail of all the animals that lived beside Looking-Glass Pond.

It was fluffier than Dilly Duck's tail… bushier than Harvey Rabbit's tail… and swooshier than everybody's!

Each morning Hazel groomed her tail and admired her reflection in the pond. "I really do have a beautiful tail!" she would say, smiling at herself in the silvery water.

Sometimes Hazel played with her friends, but it usually ended in tears.

"You splashed my lovely tail!" Hazel would shout crossly, when she played leap-frog with Webster. "You're getting my tail dirty, Harvey!" she would moan very grumpily, when they played digging.

Soon, Hazel stopped playing with her friends altogether.

"I'm far too busy brushing my tail!" she said when they came to call. "Come back some other time."

One morning as usual, Hazel was admiring her tail by the pond. Suddenly, she had a funny thought. She couldn't remember the last time she had seen her friends.

Hazel looked at her reflection in the pond. Staring back was a strange face… a cross face… a grumpy face. It was Hazel's face! Hazel couldn't believe her eyes. "No wonder my friends don't visit me any more," she cried. "I've forgotten how to smile!"

The next day Hazel called for her friends. They had such fun playing leap-frog and digging muddy holes that she forgot all about her tail. "From now on," she laughed, "the only time I'll look at my reflection is to practise smiling!"

Teddy Bear Tears

"**B**oo hoo! I want to go home!"
As a little fairy called Mavis
flew past the rubbish dump, holding her nose, she heard an
unmistakable sound coming from the other side of a very smelly pile
of rubbish.

"Oh dear. Those sound like teddy bear tears," she said to herself.
"I'd better go and see if I can help."

She flew down to take a look, and, sure enough, there amongst a heap
of old potato peelings and banana skins sat a very old, very sad teddy
indeed. Mavis sat and held his paw, while he told her tearfully what
had happened:

"My owner, Matilda, was told to clean out her room. She's terribly
messy, but she's sweet and kind," Teddy sniffed. "She threw me out with
an old blanket by mistake – she didn't realise I was tucked up having a
sleep inside it. Then some men in a big, dirty truck came and emptied
me out of the dustbin and brought me here. But I want to go home!"
And with that poor Teddy started to cry again.

"There, there," said Mavis. "I'll help to get you home. But first I'll
need two teddy bear tears." She unscrewed the lid of a little jar, and
scooped two big salty tears into it from Teddy's cheeks.

"What do you need those for?" asked Teddy, feeling rather bewildered.

"Just a little fairy magic!" said Mavis. "Now wait here, and I promise I'll be back soon." And with a wave of her wand, she disappeared.

Teddy pulled the blanket around him, and sat trying to be brave, and not to cry. He stayed like that all night, feeling cold and alone and frightened. How he wished he was back in his warm, cosy home.

Meanwhile Mavis was very busy. She flew back and forth around the neighbourhood, until she heard the sound of sobbing coming from an open window. She flew down onto the windowsill and peered inside. A little girl was lying on the bed, with her mummy sitting beside her.

"I want my teddy!" she cried.

"Well if you weren't so messy, Matilda, you wouldn't lose things," said Mummy gently.

"But I cleaned my room today!" said Matilda.

"Well, try and go to sleep now," said Mummy, kissing her goodnight, "and we'll look for Teddy in the morning."

Mavis watched as poor Matilda lay sobbing into her pillow, until at last she fell fast asleep. Then Mavis flew down from the windowsill, took out the little jar, and rubbed Teddy's tears onto Matilda's sleeping eyes. With a little fizzle of stars, the fairy magic began to work, and Matilda started to dream. She could see an old tyre, a newspaper, some tin cans, some orange peel, a blanket... wait a minute, it was her blanket, and there, wrapped inside it was her teddy, with a big tear running down his cheek! Teddy was at the rubbish dump!

The next morning, Matilda woke with a start, and remembered her dream at once. She ran downstairs to the kitchen, where Mummy was making breakfast, and told her all about it.

"We have to go to the rubbish dump! We have to save Teddy!" said Matilda.

Mummy tried to explain that it was just a dream, but Matilda wouldn't listen, she was sure she was right. So in the end they set off to take a look.

They arrived just as a big machine was scooping up the rubbish and heading for the crusher. And there, on top of the scoop, clinging to the edge, was Teddy!

Mavis appeared, hovering in the air above him.

"Don't worry, we'll save you!" she said. She waved her wand in a bright flash above Teddy. Matilda looked up and spotted him at once.

"There he is!" she cried, pointing frantically at Teddy. "He's going to be squashed! Mummy, do something, quick!" Mummy ran up to the man driving the machine, waving her arms in the air.

He stopped his machine just in time.

Soon Teddy and Matilda were reunited, and there were more tears, although this time they were happy ones. And from then on, Matilda's room was the tidiest room you have ever seen.

One Dark Night

Paws tiptoed out into the dark farmyard. Mummy had told him to stay in the barn until he was old enough to go out at night. But he was impatient. He had not gone far when something brushed past his ears. He froze as the fur on his neck began to rise. To his relief it was only a bat – there were plenty of those in the barn.

A loud hoot echoed through the trees – "Toowhit, Toowhoo!" and a great dark shape swooped down and snatched something up. "Just an owl," Paws told himself. "Some of those in the barn too. Nothing to be afraid of!" Creeping nervously on into the darkness, he wondered if this was such a good idea after all. Strange rustlings came from every corner, and he jumped as the old pig gave a loud grunt from the pigsty close by.

Then, all of a sudden, Paws froze in his tracks. Beneath the henhouse two eyes glinted in the darkness, as they came creeping towards him. This must be the fox Mummy had warned him of! But to his amazement he saw it was Mummy!

"Back to the barn!" she said sternly and Paws happily did as he was told. Maybe he would wait until he was older to go out at night, after all!

21

Every effort has been made to acknowledge the contributors to this book.
If we have made any errors, we will be pleased to rectify them in future editions.

This is a Parragon Book
This edition published in 2004

Parragon
Queen Street House
4 Queen Street
Bath BA1 1HE, UK

Design and project management by Aztec Design

Page make-up by
Mik Martin, Caroline Reeves and Kilnwood Graphics

ISBN 1-40544-207-7

Printed in Indonesia

READING TREE STARS

PICTURE DICTIONARY

CRAZY COMPOUND WORDS

night   shine   way   out

NEAT NOUNS

days   Mouse   star   summer   Mole   stars

STICKERS FOR YOU!

This
Ready Steady Read
book belongs to:

My Reading Tree!

I'm a super reader!

In memory of my
father and mother
~ A. H. B.

To all my friends and my
dearest wife, Tiziana
~ J. B.

LITTLE TIGER PRESS
An imprint of Magi Publications
1 The Coda Centre, 189 Munster Road, London SW6 6AW
www.littletigerpress.com
First published in Great Britain 2002
This edition published 2009
Text copyright © A. H. Benjamin 2002
Illustrations copyright © John Bendall-Brunello 2002
A. H. Benjamin and John Bendall-Brunello have asserted their
rights to be identified as the author and illustrator of this work
under the Copyright, Designs and Patents Act, 1988.
Printed in China
All rights reserved • ISBN 978-1-84506-879-0
3 5 7 9 10 8 6 4 2

Mouse, Mole
and the
Falling Star

A.H. Benjamin

John Bendall-Brunello

LITTLE TIGER PRESS
London

Mole and Mouse were
the best of friends.
They had fun together.

They shared everything.

They trusted each other completely,
even with their deepest secrets.

When one was sad
or not feeling well the
other was always there
to comfort him.

That's how much
they loved each other.
"I'm lucky to have
a friend like you,"
Mole would say.

"No," Mouse would
reply. "I'm lucky
to have a friend
like *you*!"

One summer evening Mole and Mouse
lay side by side on top of a hill, gazing
at the starry sky.

"Aren't stars beautiful?" sighed
Mole happily.

"Yes," said Mouse. "And magic, too.
They sometimes fall from the sky, you
know. And if you ever find a fallen star,
your wishes will come true."

"Wow!" said Mole. "Then you could
wish for anything in the world and you
would have it."

"That's right," said Mouse dreamily.
"Just imagine that!"

Mole and Mouse fell silent
for a moment, dreaming of
magic stars and all the things
they could wish for.

Just then, a shooting star zipped
across the sky. One moment it was
there, and the next it had gone.

"Did you see that?" gasped Mole,
sitting up.

"Yes, I did," cried Mouse. "It's a
fallen star, and I'm going to find it!"

Mouse scrambled to his feet and
scurried quickly down the hill.

"Wait!" called Mole, racing after him.
"It's my star! I saw it first."

"No, I saw it first!" shouted Mouse.
"It's *my* star!"

When they reached the bottom of
the hill, Mole and Mouse started
searching for the fallen star. Each
one hoped he would find it first.
But neither did.

"Perhaps the star fell in the woods," thought
Mouse. "I'll go and look for it tomorrow."

Mole stared towards the woods, too.
He was thinking exactly the same.

But they did not tell each other, and
they went back to their homes, without
even saying goodnight.

The next day before sunrise, Mole sneaked
out of his house and set off towards the woods.
A few minutes later, Mouse did the same.

Mouse and Mole spent the whole morning
in the woods, looking for the fallen star.
Once or twice, they spotted each other.
But they pretended they hadn't.

Then, towards afternoon, Mole came across a small patch of charred grass.

"Maybe this is where the star has fallen," he thought. "But someone's already taken it. It can only be Mouse!"

A little later, Mouse came across the same charred patch of grass. He thought the star had fallen there, too.

"It's gone!" he cried. "And I bet I know who's taken it. It has to be Mole!"

As darkness fell, both Mole and Mouse made their separate ways home, each feeling very angry with the other. They did not speak to each other again, except to argue.

"You stole my star!" Mole yelled.

"No, *you* stole *my* star!" Mouse yelled back.

Mole didn't trust Mouse and Mouse didn't trust Mole.

So, Mole sneaked into Mouse's
house to find the star . . .

and later on Mouse looked
through Mole's window
to see where Mole had
hidden it.

But neither found
the fallen star.

The days rolled by and summer was nearly
over. Mole and Mouse grew lonely and
miserable. They missed each other's
company, the fun they used to have
together, the secrets they had shared.
They even missed the sad moments.

"Mole can keep the star if he wants,"
thought Mouse. "All I want is my
friend back."

   "If I had never seen that star,
Mouse would still be my friend,"
thought Mole.

   Soon the fallen star became just
a sad memory – until one day . . .

Mouse was climbing up the hill when he spotted a golden leaf, swirling and twirling in the air.

"It's the fallen star!" he cried. "Mole must have lost it. I'll catch it for him."

Not far away Mole noticed Mouse chasing after something that looked very like a star.

"It's Mouse's star," he thought. "I'll help him catch it."

Up and up the hill ran Mole and
Mouse, until they reached the top.
But the leaf was already high in the sky,
glimmering in the autumn sunshine.
It swayed this way and that, as if waving
goodbye, and then vanished altogether.

"The star has gone back to the sky,"
said Mouse.

"That's where it belongs," said Mole.

"Maybe it's for the best," sighed Mouse.

"I'm sure it is," agreed Mole.

There was a moment's silence.

"Anyway, we don't need a star.
We have each other," said Mouse.

"Of course we have," agreed Mole.

They gave each other a big hug,
then they lay back on top of the
hill, feeling the wind. With their
arms and legs stretched out, they
looked just like two furry stars.

Picture Dictionary

Look at the words below and put the correct
picture stickers next to each word.

ball   leaf

moon   sandwich

 Have you got these right?
Then put a star on your reading tree!

Drawing

Draw a picture in the frame
for each word below.

flower   spade   star

 Did you draw all three pictures?
Add another star to your reading tree!

Perfect Plurals

A **noun** is a naming word – a person, place or thing.
A **plural noun** shows there is more than one person,
place or thing. An "s" at the end of a noun often
means that it is plural.

E.g. shoe – shoes

Circle the plural nouns in the sentences below.

1) They trusted each other completely,
   even with their deepest secrets.
2) A few minutes later, Mouse did the same.
3) They even missed the sad moments.
4) With their arms and legs stretched out,
   they looked just like two furry stars.

 Did you get these right?
Then add a star to your reading tree!

Crazy Compound Words

When two short words join together,
they form a **compound word.**

Put the correct word stickers next to the words below to
make a compound word. Then write the new compound
word on the line. We've done the first one for you.

1) every + (thing) = _everything_

2) good + = _____

3) any + = _____

4) sun + = _____

5) with + = _____

Did you get these right? Great!
Then add another star to your reading tree!

Opposite Words

Match the words on the left to their **opposites** on the right. We've done the first one for you.

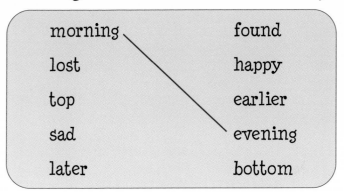

morning   found

lost   happy

top   earlier

sad   evening

later   bottom

Did you match the words with their opposites? Then add a star to your reading tree!

Sentence Order

All stories are made up of **sentences**.
Place the sentences below in the order they appear in the story by adding numbers to the boxes.

☐ Mole and Mouse were the best of friends.

☐ Up and up the hill ran Mole and Mouse, until they reached the top.

☐ They had fun together.

Did you get these right? Remember to add another star to your reading tree.

Neat Nouns

A **noun** is a naming word – a person, place or thing.
Add the missing nouns to the sentences below
with the word stickers.

days – Mouse – star – summer – Mole – stars

1) "Aren't _____ beautiful?" sighed

Mole happily.

2) But neither found the fallen _____.

3) _____ and _____ grew

lonely and miserable.

4) The _____ rolled by and _____

was nearly over.

Did you get all the nouns right?
Add the last star to your reading tree.